HOWARD HELPS OUT

Stories and Pictures
by Colin West

An I

D1471948

First published in Great Britain 1993 in Young Lions
3 5 7 9 10 8 6 4 2

Young Lions is an imprint of the Children's Division,
part of HarperCollins Publishers Ltd,
77/85 Fulham Palace Road, Hammersmith,
London W6 8JB

ISBN 0 00 674469 9

Printed and bound in Great Britain by
HarperCollins Book Manufacturing, Glasgow

Contents

Howard's Who's Who   4

Howard Helps Out   8

Howard and the Peanut Butter   24

Howard Gets Wet   40

Howard and the New Hat   54

HOWARD'S WHO'S WHO

This is Howard.
His hobbies include
roller skating,
watching TV
and doing difficult

jigsaws. Favourite food: hamburgers.
Favourite drink: banana milkshakes.
Wants to be: a traffic warden.

Alice is Howard's
sister.
She likes collecting
things: pebbles,
china ornaments
and Anything Pink.
She plays tennis
and basketball.
She doesn't get on
too well with Howard.

Howard's parents have been married for seventeen whole years. His mum likes tinkering with cars and watching keep-fit videos. His dad likes gardening and D.I.Y. He grows all his own vegetables.

So that's Howard's family, but what about his friends?

Ronald is Howard's
best friend.
He likes dressing up,
waterski-ing and
old Tarzan movies.
He plays the violin
pretty well for
a rhino.

Lucy is Howard's
special friend.
She's a tapir,
and she likes
pop music,
dancing and
weight training.
When she grows
up she hopes to
run a guest house.

Englebert
lives next door
to Howard.
He's only little
and likes playing
around.

So that's Howard's family and friends.
Now let's have some stories about
them all ...

HOWARD HELPS OUT

Howard was feeling in a helpful mood.
He saw his mum weeding the
vegetable plot.
"Hey, Mum, can I help out?" he asked.
His mother remembered the last time
Howard helped out.
He'd trodden all over the turnips,
and pulled up the potatoes by mistake.

8

"No thanks, Howard," she answered.
"I'm almost finished now."

"OK, Mum," said Howard, and he went
away.

Howard was disappointed,
but at the front gate his father
was painting the fence.

"Hey, Dad," said Howard, "can I help out?"

His dad remembered the last time Howard helped out.

He'd splattered yellow paint all over the floor and he'd left sticky footprints all over the hall.

"Not really, Howard," he replied. "I've nearly finished now."

"OK, Dad," said Howard, and he went away.

Howard was quite fed up now,
but at the window he saw his sister
Alice tidying her room.
"Hey, Alice, can I help out?" he asked.
Alice remembered the last time
Howard helped out.
He'd dropped her favourite china vase,
and messed up her collection of shells.

"Not likely, Howard," she replied.
"You're so clumsy, I wouldn't let you
help out if you were the last hippo
on earth!"

Howard was really hurt now.

"OK Alice," he sighed, and went away.

Howard walked down to the river
and sat under his favourite tree.
"No one wants my help!"
he moaned to himself.
After a while, little Englebert Alligator,
who lived next door, came by.
"Hello, Howard!" he said excitedly.
"Come and join me on a hike!"

Howard thought for a moment.
"You're a long way from home," he
said. "Do your mum and dad know
where you are?"
Englebert let out a laugh.
"No chance!" he replied. "My mum
wanted me to help out with the
cooking, and my dad wanted me to
help out with the dishes. So I gave
them the slip and came down here
for a hike!"
"But don't you think they'll be
worried?" asked Howard.

"Oh, I never thought of that,"
confessed Englebert.
"I think I'd better take you home!"
said Howard.

He took the little alligator
by the hand and led him
through the woods back home.
It was a bit scary at times.

When they arrived home,
Englebert's mother and father
were overjoyed.
"Look who's here!"
they squealed.
They had been
looking for Englebert
all afternoon.

"Thanks so much for bringing
Englebert home safely," said
Mr Alligator.
"That's all right," said Howard.
"I always like to help out
whenever I can."
"In that case," said Mrs Alligator,
"you must stay and help us eat
this pumpkin pie I've made."
So Howard did.
It was delicious.

HOWARD AND THE PEANUT BUTTER

One Monday, Howard and his sister
Alice were having an argument
in the supermarket.
It was about peanut butter.
Alice wanted the smooth kind, and
Howard wanted the crunchy.

Their mum finally lost patience.
"If you can't decide between you,
you can both go without," she told
them. And she didn't buy any at all.

25

At home that evening,
Howard felt like a snack.
He looked in the fridge.

No peanut butter!
He remembered the quarrel
earlier that day.
If only Alice hadn't wanted
the smooth kind,
he could have had a peanut
butter sandwich.

Howard looked around to see
what he could have instead.
There was cheese and fruit.
But he didn't feel like cheese or fruit.
Then Howard looked in the cupboard.
There were baked beans and spaghetti.
But he didn't feel like
baked beans or spaghetti
But then Howard saw,
right at the back,
there was a jar of peanut butter.
"Hooray! I've found some at last!"
he chortled.

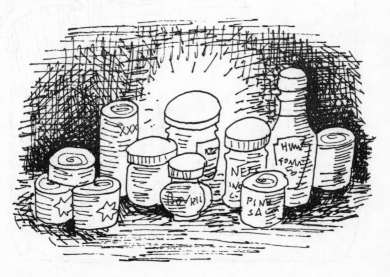

There wasn't much left
in the jar, though.
Just enough for one sandwich,
Howard reckoned.
He unscrewed the top.
Then Howard noticed something.
He could see it wasn't his favourite
crunchy kind, it was the smooth.
Now, to be honest, Howard didn't mind
the smooth kind too much.
In fact, he rather liked it.

Howard started to spread some
on a slice of brown bread.
Just then, Alice came into the kitchen.

Alice had fancied a snack too.
She looked in the fridge.
No peanut butter!
Alice remembered the quarrel earlier
that day too.
If only Howard hadn't wanted
the crunchy kind,
she could have had a peanut
butter sandwich.

Alice looked around
to see what she could
eat instead.

There were biscuits and crisps.

But she didn't feel like
biscuits or crisps.
There was celery and carrots.

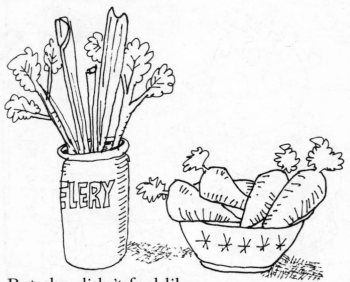

But she didn't feel like
celery or carrots.

Alice turned round and
saw Howard about to bite
his peanut butter sandwich.
"What's that?" she screamed.
"It's peanut butter!" Howard replied.
"But it's the smooth kind.
The kind you don't like!" Alice yelled.
"I've changed my mind!" replied Howard.
And he took a big bite.

Yuk!
Howard could
hardly believe it.

It tasted awful.
It was nasty
and hot.

He just about
managed to
swallow a
mouthful.

Alice looked on.
Howard took another bite.
It was terrible.
But he kept on eating
till every bit of the sandwich
was gone.

38

That night Howard felt ill.
He had to drink seven glasses of water.
When Howard's mum cleared up
the kitchen things,
she picked up the empty jar
from the table.
"Now that's funny," she said.
"Who could have finished up
the mustard like that?"

She never found out that Howard
had thought the jar of mustard
was a jar of peanut butter.

It was raining.
Howard had to go out
to meet his friend Ronald.
He hated getting wet.
"I'll just wait a minute
and the rain might stop,"
Howard said to himself.
He waited a minute.
But it was still raining.

"I'll just go and make myself a
milkshake. It might have stopped
raining by then," Howard thought.
So he went and made himself
a milkshake.
But it was still raining.

"I'll just go and get my things ready,"
thought Howard.
Howard put on his waterproof mac
and fetched his bag and umbrella.
It was still raining.
"Oh well, here goes!" he thought.

Howard walked down the road,
trying not to get wet.
Suddenly he saw his friend Lucy
hurrying home with some shopping.
Lucy waved at Howard.

And Howard waved back.
Oops! Howard almost stepped
in a puddle.
"That was close!" he thought.
He hated getting wet.

Soon Howard met Ronald who
was waiting at the corner.
Ronald looked very wet.
"Why are you so late?"
he asked Howard.
"I tried waiting for the rain to stop,"
replied Howard.

"Do you still want to go?"
asked Ronald.
"I suppose so," said Howard.
So they set off together.

As they walked along,
it stopped raining.
After a while the sun came out.
Howard felt hot in his mac.
His umbrella was getting heavy.
"Nearly there!" said Ronald.
The sun was shining brightly now.
Howard felt sticky.
But he plodded on.

49

At last they got there.
They had reached the lake.
"Yippee!" cried Ronald.
Howard was sweating a lot.
The two friends changed into
their costumes.
They were glad to get out of
their hot sticky clothes.

Howard and Ronald jumped in.
The water was cool and refreshing.
Howard felt better.
"Getting wet is good fun sometimes!"
he thought.

Lucy, Howard's special friend, had
a new hat.
It was made of straw and had
flowers round the brim.
She was very proud of her hat.

Lucy walked up to Howard.
"Notice anything new?" she asked.
Howard scratched his head.
"You've got a new dress?" he
asked hopefully.
"No, silly!" replied Lucy.

Howard scratched his head again.
"A new pair of shoes?" he suggested.
"No, Howard, not shoes!" sighed Lucy.

Howard scratched his head again.
"I've got it!" he said suddenly.
"You've got a new handbag!"
"Howard, you really are the limit!"
shrieked Lucy.
And she stormed off in a huff.

At home that afternoon, Lucy stared
at her new hat.
The flowers looked rather wilted.
"What's the matter, dear?"
her mum asked.
Lucy told her how Howard hadn't
noticed her new hat.

Meanwhile, Howard was worried
he'd upset Lucy.
But he still couldn't work out
what was new about her.
"I'll take some flowers round to
show I'm sorry," he thought.

Howard picked some flowers
from the front garden.

Howard went to Lucy's house
on top of the hill.
He knocked on the door.
Lucy's mother answered.

60

"Hello, Howard!" she said.
"Hello," replied Howard shyly.
"I've brought Lucy some flowers."
"How lovely!" said Lucy's mum.
She invited Howard in.

They went into the front room,
where Lucy was sitting.
"Howard's brought some flowers
for your hat," her mum said.
Lucy looked delighted.

Howard realised it was Lucy's hat
which was new.
How could he have missed it?

Howard and Lucy spent some time
decorating her hat with the daisies.
It looked better than ever.

"Wow! Even I would notice
a hat like that!" said Howard.
And Lucy laughed more
than she'd ever laughed before.